Fairy
In Waiting

Also by Sophie Kinsella

Finding Audrey

THE SHOPAHOLIC SERIES

Shopaholic to the Stars
Confessions of a Shopaholic
Shopaholic Takes Manhattan
Shopaholic Ties the Knot
Shopaholic & Sister
Shopaholic & Baby
Mini Shopaholic

OTHER NOVELS

Surprise Me
My Not So Perfect Life
I've Got Your Number
Can You Keep a Secret?
The Undomestic Goddess
Remember Me?
Twenties Girl
Wedding Night

SOPHIE KINSELLA

Fairy In Waiting

The sequel to Fairy Mom and Me

illustrated by
Marta Kissi

Delacorte
Press

Text copyright © 2018 by Sophie Kinsella
Jacket art copyright © 2018 by Marta Kissi
Interior illustrations copyright © 2018 by Marta Kissi

Visit us on the Web! rhcbooks.com

Educators and librarians, for a variety of teaching tools, visit us at
RHTeachersLibrarians.com

Library of Congress Cataloging-in-Publication Data is available upon request.
ISBN 978-1-5247-6991-8 (trade) |
ISBN 978-1-5247-6922-5 (ebook)

Printed in the United States of America
10 9 8 7 6 5 4 3 2 1
First U.S. Edition

For Phoebe and Saskia

Contents

Meet Fairy Mom and Me

Hi. My name is Ella Brook and I live in a town called Cherrywood with my mom, my dad and my baby brother, Ollie. I have blue eyes and dark brown hair. My best friends at school are Tom and Lenka. My worst enemy is Zoe. She lives next door and she's my Not-Best Friend. She is the meanest girl ever. She looks mean even when she smiles.

Everything in my life seems normal, but my family has a special secret that I'm not allowed to tell anyone, even my friends. My mom looks like any other mom . . . but she's not a regular mom. Because she can turn into a fairy.

All she has to do is stamp her feet three times, clap her hands, wiggle her behind and say, "Marshmallow," . . . and POOF! She's Fairy Mom. Then if she says, "Toffee apple," she's just Mom again.

My Aunty Jo and Granny are fairies too. They can all fly and turn invisible and do real magic. And Mom and Aunty Jo also

have a really cool wand called a Computawand V5. It has magic powers and a computer screen *and* an Extra-Fast Magic button. And it has Fairy Apps and Fairy Mail and Fairy Games.

The problem is that Mom . . . well . . . she is not that good at doing magic spells, even though she works really hard at her magic lessons

on FairyTube with Fairy Fenella. But one day she's going to get everything right. And one day, when I'm grown up, I'll be a fairy like she is. I'll have sparkly wings and my own Computawand.

Until then, Mom says I just have to wait. So that's what I am. A Fairy in Waiting.

Fairy Spell #1

MONKERIDOO!

Fairy Mom
and the Monkey Business

One day I was watching Fairy Mom learning magic from Fenella, her Fairy Tutor on FairyTube. She was learning a weather spell called Raineridoo. I was watching from under a regular umbrella while my mom practiced with one that floated in the air. I really wanted a magic umbrella too, but at least I got to watch.

"You can use lots of different spells to stop the rain," Fenella said on the computer screen. "Try 'Normeridoo' with the code four-five-two. It's a very useful spell."

My mom pressed 4-5-2 on her

Computawand and said, "Normeridoo!" and the rain stopped instantly.

After my mom had finished the lesson and turned back into a regular mom, I sighed.

"What's wrong, Ella?" she asked.

"I'm tired of being a Fairy in Waiting," I said. "I want to be a *real* fairy and do *real* magic and save the day."

Mom laughed. "Every little fairy girl feels that way," she said. "I promise you'll get your chance when you're older. Now, what can we do to cheer you up?"

"Go roller-skating with Lenka and Tom?" I said. "They're meeting at the park."

"Oh, I'm sorry," Mom said. "I forgot that we're going to lunch with Dad's boss, Mr. Lee. But that will be fun too!"

I didn't believe her. Then Dad came in.

"Time to get ready for the lunch," he said. "Mr. Lee is very important, so we must make a good impression."

Now I *knew* the lunch wouldn't be fun.

I put on my best dress, and my mom did my hair. She was trying to do French braids, but Ollie kept pulling her arm and she kept dropping pieces of hair.

"Be *good,* Ollie!" I said, but I don't think Ollie knows what "good" means.

"Right," Dad said, walking in. He was wearing his fanciest suit and a blue polka-dot tie. "Are we all ready? Let's get in the car."

Mom reached for a ribbon, then dropped a piece of my hair again. "Oh, I'm sorry," she said. "I think I need some help." She stamped her feet three times, clapped her hands, wiggled her behind and said, "Marshmallow," . . . and POOF! She was a fairy.

When my mom turns into a fairy, she still looks like herself but even more beautiful. The sunlight was gleaming on her wings, and her dress was all sparkly and her silver crown shimmered.

She waved her Computawand, pressed a code—*bleep-bleep-bloop*—and said, "Braidseridoo!"

A moment later, my hair was in the neatest, most beautiful braids I'd ever seen, tied with red ribbons in bows.

"Mom!" I said. "These are so pretty! You're the best! Look, Dad!"

But when I looked at Dad, I gasped. Normally he has short brown hair. But now he had long brown braids with pink bows.

I turned and saw that Mom had long

braids too. Even Ollie had long braids. We all had braids.

"What?" Dad said in horror when he saw his braids in the mirror. "*What* have you done to me? I look like Ella!"

"Oops," Mom said. "I don't know how

that happened. I'm sure I said the right spell."

She quickly scrolled through the Spell App on her Computawand, then stopped and said, *"Here* it is." She pressed in a code and said, "Haireridoo!"

Suddenly we all had normal hair again.

But Dad was still frowning. "This lunch is important," he said. "I don't want anything to go wrong. So I have a special rule for today: no magic."

"No magic?" Mom said.

"That's right," Dad said. He sounded very firm. *"No magic."*

On the way to Mr. Lee's house, Mom didn't do any magic. Even when the GPS system wasn't working and we got lost, Mom didn't do a spell. She just asked a nice lady on the street for directions instead.

When we got to Mr. Lee's house, we saw that it was very big, with a huge garden and woods in the backyard. Mrs. Lee showed me, Mom and Ollie the garden while Dad and Mr. Lee were talking.

In the backyard there was a wooden perch for a bird, but it was empty.

"Do you have a pet bird?" I asked, and Mrs. Lee started blinking. She had tears in her eyes.

"Oh no!" Mom said "Are you all right, Mrs. Lee? What's happened?"

"I have a parrot called Ben," said Mrs. Lee. "I love him very much. But he's flown away! He's never done that before. I think he was getting bored." She looked even sadder. "Anyway, why don't you two stay out here and enjoy the fresh air while I finish cooking lunch. It's almost ready."

Mrs. Lee took a tissue from her pocket and blew her nose and went into the kitchen to finish cooking lunch.

When Mrs. Lee walked inside, I could smell something yummy cooking. But I couldn't help feeling sorry for her. Mrs. Lee was a very kind lady, and if I had a parrot as a pet, I wouldn't want it to fly away.

"Do you want to play, Ella?" Mom asked.

"No," I said. "I want to find Mrs. Lee's parrot for her."

"I agree," Mom said. "Let's go look."

We searched all the flower beds and trees. But we couldn't see a parrot anywhere. Then we looked at the wood at the edge of the garden.

"Maybe Ben flew into the woods," I said. "We'll *never* find him."

"It's no use," Mom said. "We'll have to use magic."

"But Dad said we can't," I reminded her.

"Right." Mom thought for a moment. "I think he meant 'No magic unless there's a lost parrot.' I'll be super careful. No one will know."

"Mom, can I do the magic?" I begged. "Please?"

Mom smiled but shook her head no. "You know you're a Fairy in Waiting, Ella. But you can still help me. Make sure no one can see us."

I checked carefully, but we were alone. Then Mom stamped her feet three times,

clapped her hands, wiggled her behind and said, "Marshmallow," . . . and POOF! She was a fairy.

She pressed her Computawand—*bleep-bleep-bloop*—and said, "Beneridoo! Finderidoo! Flyeridoo!" Then she grabbed my hand.

The next minute we were flying through the air. It felt really cold and whooshy. The

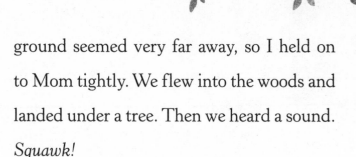

ground seemed very far away, so I held on to Mom tightly. We flew into the woods and landed under a tree. Then we heard a sound. *Squawk!*

"The parrot is in the tree!" I said. "We found Ben! What do we do now?"

"We can't startle him," Mom said, "or he may fly away. I'll fly up very slowly and try to catch him."

I watched her rise up into the air very

quietly, but then I heard that sound again: *squawk!*

"Ben saw me," Mom called down, "and he's flown to another branch. He's a very sneaky parrot. Ella, your time to help has come. Are you ready?"

"Yes!" I said. "What do I do?"

"I think you should climb the tree. Between us, we can catch him."

I looked up at the tree. It was very tall, with big branches.

"Don't worry, Ella," Mom said, her eyes twinkling. "I'll give you some magic help. You'll need super-strong legs."

"Okay!" I said, feeling excited. Maybe I couldn't do magic spells yet—but I could still catch Ben and save the day.

Mom pressed a code on her Compu-tawand—*bleep-bleep-bloop*. "Climberidoo!" she shouted.

I looked at my legs to see if they were getting stronger yet. They *were* changing. But they were also getting very brown and hairy. My arms were brown and hairy too.

I turned to Mom for help, but then I screamed. She had turned into a monkey—which meant I was one too! Ollie stared up at us with his big blue eyes.

"Mom!" I said in a monkey voice. "You've turned us both into monkeys!"

"Oops," Mom said—and she had a monkey voice too. "I don't know how *that* happened." She put down the Computawand, jumped up on a branch and swung by her tail. "Hey, look what I can do."

"I want to try!" I said. "Monkeridoo!" I

jumped up too, and we both swung by our tails. I hurried to the top of the tallest tree, but I still couldn't see Ben the parrot. Then I leaped to another tree and swung by my tail again. Being a monkey was fun.

Suddenly we heard Mrs. Lee calling for us. I gasped.

"Mom, it's lunchtime!" I said. "Quick, change us back to people!"

"Where did my Computawand go?" Mom asked. "And where's Ollie?"

Then we saw him. He was crawling off through the woods, holding the Computawand.

"Oh no!" Mom cried. "Chase him!"

We chased Ollie on our monkey paws, and Mom had almost reached him when Mrs. Lee appeared through the trees. Mom dived behind a bush and pulled me with her. I was breathing very fast. I didn't want Mrs. Lee to see us and freak out because there were monkeys in her backyard.

"Hello, young man," Mrs. Lee said to Ollie. "What are you doing out here all alone? Did you wander off?"

She looked around for Mom and me, but we kept very still behind the bush.

"Weezi-weezi-weezi!" Ollie said, pointing toward the bush, but Mrs. Lee couldn't understand him. I was very glad Ollie couldn't talk.

"That's a very stylish phone," Mrs. Lee said, and she took the Computawand from him. Luckily, it had turned itself off, so now it looked like a normal phone.

"This must belong to your mom. Let's go and have some lunch." And she carried Ollie away, toward the lunch table in the garden.

Mom and I looked at each other. This was awful! What could we do? We were monkeys, and Mrs. Lee had the Computawand.

"We need to get the Computawand back," Mom said. "Otherwise we'll be monkeys forever. Follow me, Ella. And when we see the others, pretend to be a real monkey. Do monkey things. Go bananas."

"Go bananas?" I said. "Act wild on purpose?"

"Yes," Mom said, and her monkey eyes twinkled. "Just this once you can get into as much trouble as you want."

We snuck through the garden and up to the lunch table. Mrs. Lee was the first to see us, and she gasped.

Mom leaped onto the table. "Ooh-ooh-ooh-ah-ah!" she cried, and threw a bread roll at Mr. Lee. Then she put her monkey fingers up Dad's nose, and he sprang from the table. Mr. and Mrs. Lee screamed.

I jumped on the table and screeched. I ran up and down. Then I played with Mrs. Lee's

hair and stuck out my tongue at her. Mr. Lee
jumped up and tried to catch me.

"Help!" Mrs. Lee cried. "Did they come
from the zoo?"

"Maybe the circus!" Mr. Lee yelled back.

I started throwing salad around. Then
I saw Dad. He was looking straight at me.
He looked at the Computawand on
the table, and then at Mom.

He knew it was us.

"Ooh-ooh-ooh-ah-ah," I said to him. I pointed to the Computawand with my monkey paw. What I meant was *Give us the Computawand quick, Dad!*

Dad understood. He picked up the Computawand and waved it at Mom as if he was trying to shoo her away.

"Go away, monkey," he said. "Go away."

Mom grabbed the Computawand and ran away.

Mrs. Lee gasped. "That monkey stole your phone!"

"Don't worry," Dad said. "I'll chase it."

Mom and I ran off into the woods, and Dad ran after us. He looked very mad.

"I thought I said no magic," Dad said. "That's what we agreed. All I wanted was to have a nice, simple lunch. And now look— you're monkeys."

"I'm sorry," Mom said. "We were trying to find Mrs. Lee's lost parrot. I'll change us back. No problemo."

She waved her Computawand, pressed a code—*bleep-bleep-bloop*—and said, "Un-monkeridoo!"

I could feel the spell working. My hairy legs were changing and I was getting taller. A lot taller. And bigger.

"What did you do?" Dad shouted.

I looked down and gasped. I wasn't a monkey anymore. I had tusks! And great big feet! I was an elephant! And so was Mom!

I picked an apple off a tree with my trunk and gave it to Dad. Being an elephant was fun too.

But then I started to worry that Mom couldn't change me back into a girl. How could I be an elephant forever? I wouldn't be able to go to school. I would sit on my chair and it would break. I decided I really, *really* didn't want to be an elephant.

"Mom!" I said in a trumpety elephant voice. "Do another spell!"

"Oops," Mom said, and her voice was trumpety too. "Sorry

about that. Let me try again." She tried to use her trunk to press in another code, but the Computawand fell to the ground. "This is tricky," she said. "How do elephants press buttons?"

"They don't do magic," Dad said with a sigh. He picked up the Computawand and held it out in front of Mom. This time, she managed to press the code—*bleep-bleep-bloop.*

"Unelephanteridoo!" she trumpeted.

The magic was working again. I was getting shorter and shorter. I wasn't an elephant anymore . . . but I wasn't a girl either.

I was a penguin. And so was Mom.

"Penguins?" Dad said, staring at me and Mom. "*Penguins?* This is ridiculous!"

"I don't know how *that* happened," Mom said in a penguin bark.

I tried to walk to Mom, but I could only waddle. I *really* didn't want to be a penguin.

I would have to go and live in the snow and only eat fish.

"Hello?" I could hear Mrs. Lee calling through the woods. "Are you there? Are you all right?"

We all looked at each other. I tried to waddle to Mom.

"My spells aren't working!" Mom said to
me. "I don't know *what* to do."

Then I had an idea.

"Mom . . . ," I began.

"Not now, Ella!"

"But I know which spell you should use!"
I said.

"Use the Normeridoo spell!" I said.
"Code four-five-two. Remember?"

"Yes!" Mom shouted. "What a good
idea!"

She waved her Computawand, tapped out
the numbers 4-5-2 with the end of her flipper
and said, "Normeridoo! Please! Please work!"

I could feel myself getting bigger. My flippers became arms. My beak became a nose. My hair came back. I was a girl again.

"Thank goodness," Dad said. He grabbed me and Mom and gave us a hug. "Now, absolutely *no more magic*."

"Ella, you are a wonderful Fairy in Waiting," Mom said. "You saved the day for everyone."

I felt all light and happy. I *had* saved the day!

"Thank goodness for Ella," Dad said, and he gave me an extra-big hug. "Now can we have lunch like a normal family? Just for once?"

"Of course!" Mom said. "Toffee apple." And she changed back to normal Mom.

At that moment, Mrs. Lee appeared through the trees. She looked very confused to see us all together.

"Hello!" she said. "There you all are! What's going on?"

"Um . . . ," Mom said

"Well . . . ," Dad said.

"*Squawk!*" came a voice from above. And down from the tree flew Ben the parrot. He was red and green, and he flew straight to

Mrs. Lee and sat on her shoulder.

"Ben!" cried Mrs. Lee. "You found my Ben! Thank you so much!" She stroked his head and he rubbed his beak against her. "Now come and have lunch," she said to us. "You earned it!"

We walked to the table and sat down with Ollie and Mr. Lee.

"You'll never believe it," Mr. Lee said, "but we just had two monkeys in the garden!"

"No!" Mom said, sounding very surprised. "Real monkeys?"

"Yes!" said Mrs. Lee. "They were starting trouble, but they were funny too. I'm so sorry you missed them, Ella. Maybe they'll be back. I have no idea where they came from. . . ."

"Well, I *don't* hope they come back," Dad said, smiling at me. "I don't want any more monkey business."

Just then, Ben landed on my shoulder. His claws were sharp, but it didn't hurt. It felt funny, having a parrot on my shoulder.

"I'm going to buy Ben some parrot toys," said Mrs. Lee. "Then he won't be bored."

"*Squawk!*" Ben said into my ear. He looked at me as though he was wondering why I wasn't a monkey anymore.

I had thought this lunch would be boring, but it was so much fun. I couldn't wait to tell Tom and Lenka about the parrot. Maybe one day I could have a parrot as a pet. And we could play pirates or hide-and-seek together.

After lunch I did some drawing in my book. I drew Ben in the tree, with his red and green feathers. And as I drew, I thought about being a monkey with furry legs. I thought about being an elephant with a long gray trunk, and a penguin with flippers. And I thought that what I *really* liked being, most of all, was a girl.

Fairy Spell #2

STOPERIDOO!

You Can't Stop a
Magic Wardrobe

One day, we were out shopping when Mom stopped dead and said, "Wow! That's amazing!"

I looked around quickly, in case it was something *really* amazing, like a bathtub full of jelly beans or a real live robot. But it was only an antiques shop with a big clock in the window. Antiques *aren't* what I'd call amazing. They are old furniture and things that smell dusty and don't work. You can't touch them or sit on them or play with them, even if it's a doll or a rocking horse.

But Mom says that antiques are special, like treasure. She loves old cupboards and vases and pictures. Dad doesn't. He calls antiques "junk" and stands at the door of the shop, looking at his phone.

We all followed Mom into the shop and watched her admire the clock. Then she spotted some candlesticks and plates. Everything looked boring to me, especially the plates. Plates are only interesting if they have yummy food on them, like spaghetti.

Then Mom cried out again, "Wow! That's amazing!"

By now, she was at the back of the shop, looking at a big wooden wardrobe. It had little legs and pictures of trees painted on it.

It actually *was* amazing. I had never seen a wardrobe like it before. I looked at the pictures and wondered who had painted them.

"It's beautiful," Mom said. "We have to buy this."

Dad looked up from his phone. "It's very big," he said. "And the door is falling off."

"We'll fix it," Mom said.

Dad looked at the wardrobe again. He didn't seem happy. "Do we really need this?" he said.

"We'll keep our extra clothes in it," Mom said. "It's fabulous."

When Mom says things are fabulous, we always buy them.

When the wardrobe was delivered, it seemed even bigger than it had in the store. The men heaved it in through the door and up to the guest room, while Mom followed them, saying, "Isn't it beautiful?"

"Now we must fix this door," Mom said when the men left. She looked around. "Where did Dad go?"

A text beeped on her phone. Mom read it and looked a little bit mad.

"Dad has suddenly decided to take Ollie to the supermarket," she said. "Well, that's okay. I'll fix the door myself."

Mom got out the toolbox. She put a scarf around her hair. She made herself a cup of tea. She took out the screwdriver and looked at it before putting it down. "Magic is better," she said. She stamped her feet three times, clapped her hands, wiggled her behind and said, "Marshmallow," . . . and POOF! She was a fairy.

I was excited to see Fairy Mom fix the wardrobe, but I hoped nothing would go wrong.

"Have you ever done any fixing spells before?" I asked her.

"Actually," Mom said, "I am very good at fixing spells. I got a gold in my Fixing and Building Spells test." She pointed her Computawand at the wardrobe, pressed a code—*bleep-bleep-bloop*—and said, "Menderidoo!"

The wardrobe door came to life and made itself straight. The screwdriver floated into the air and fixed it with a screw. The door was perfect again.

"Yay!" I said, and clapped my hands.

"There," Mom said. "Good as new. What a beautiful wardrobe! Let's put all our winter clothes in it."

We found our sweaters and put them into the wardrobe before closing the doors. But within seconds, the doors opened and the sweaters flew out again, landing on the carpet.

Mom and I stared at the clothes on the floor.

"Did those sweaters just fly out of the wardrobe by themselves?" Mom asked.

I was confused too.

We tried putting the sweaters in the ward-robe again, but they flew out a second time. This time, one landed on Mom's head.

"Mom!" I said. "The wardrobe is magic!"

"Oh no!" Mom said. "My spell must have been too strong. Let me fix it." She got out her Computawand, but before she could use it, we heard something coming from the wardrobe.

"Itchy," said a very small, squeaky voice.

"Itchy?" Mom asked. "What does that mean?"

"I think it means the sweaters," I said. "The sweaters are too itchy."

I felt sorry for the wardrobe. Itchy sweaters are horrible.

"This is ridiculous!" Mom said. "It's a wardrobe, not a person!" She pointed her wand at the wardrobe and said, "Stoperidoo!

Now it will become normal again."

But the wardrobe did not become normal again.

"Itchy!" it said. **"No sweaters!"**

Then it started walking to the door on its little legs.

"Mom!" I said. "It's a walking, talking wardrobe!"

"Stop right there!" Mom said, pointing her wand at the wardrobe. **"Stoperidoo!"**

But the wardrobe didn't stop. It walked along the hall and started going down the stairs. *Thump, crash, thump.* Mom ran after it, calling **"Stoperidoo! Stayeridoo! Stilleridoo!"** But it still didn't work.

Mom tried grabbing the wardrobe, but it

59

was too heavy. It marched out the back door into the garden. Then it found our inflatable pool and started kicking its legs, making big splashes.

"Stop that!" Mom shouted. **"Stoperidoo!"** The wardrobe laughed a squeaky laugh— **"Hee-hee-hee!"**—and splashed even harder.

"None of my spells are working," Mom said. "I think this wardrobe has its own kind of magic." She walked up to the wardrobe and looked at it hard. "Tell me the truth. Did I turn you into a magic wardrobe or were you magic all along?"

"Magic!" said the wardrobe in its tiny, squeaky voice. **"I'm a magic wardrobe!"**

Suddenly it grew a pair of wooden arms, with wooden hands. It waved at me, and I laughed.

"Look, Mom!" I said. "It's got arms!"

Mom sighed. "We can't have a magic wardrobe," she said. "We'll have to get rid of it."

I couldn't believe it.

"But I love the wardrobe!" I said. "It's fun!"

"Ella, we can't keep a magic wardrobe," Mom said. "It will be too much trouble. I'll lock it in the shed, and then we'll sell it."

When Dad came home, he and Mom had a talk. Then Dad talked very sternly to the wardrobe and tied a rope around one of its legs. He made it walk to the shed and locked the door. I was very sad. Before I went to bed, I ran to the shed. I looked through the window at the wardrobe.

"Good night," I said. "I wish you hadn't gotten into so much trouble today. Then maybe Mom and Dad would let you stay."

* * *

Later that night I dreamed about a fire engine. The sirens sounded like **"Waaah, waaah, waaah."**

When I woke up I realized it wasn't a dream. There was a real noise in the house. It sounded like **"Waaah, waaah, waaah."**

I got out of bed and went to the door. I peeked outside and saw Mom and Dad in their dressing gowns. They had been woken up too.

"What is that noise?" Dad asked.

"It's coming from the back door," Mom said.

We all hurried downstairs, and Dad

opened the back door. Outside, on the doorstep, was the magic wardrobe. It was crying very loudly: **"Waaah, waaah, waaah!"**

"It wants to come in," I said. "It's lonely. Poor wardrobe."

"How did it get out?" Dad asked.

"It has to go back in the shed," Mom said, and the wardrobe cried, **"Waaah!"** even more loudly. Up and down our street, lights were going on in houses. The wardrobe was waking everyone up.

"Please can the wardrobe come in?" I begged. "It sounds so sad."

"All right!" Mom said to the wardrobe. "You can come in for one night. But *that's it*."

The wardrobe hurried into the house on its little legs. It went to stand next to the grandfather clock.

"Night-night," I said to the wardrobe. The wardrobe gave me a hug with its wooden arms and I hugged it back.

"Now, be good," Mom said, and she wagged her finger at the wardrobe.

"Good," the wardrobe said in its squeaky voice. **"Good, good, good."**

Mom, Dad and I went back upstairs to bed.

"Well," Dad said, "let's hope we get some sleep tonight."

But we didn't get much sleep. Later that night, I was in the middle of a dream where

I was flying with butterflies, when I heard a loud noise: *crash!*

I woke up instantly and jumped out of bed. I knew it was the wardrobe getting into trouble again. Maybe it was running around, or maybe it was trying to play with the normal furniture. Mom and Dad would be very mad if they were woken up again, and they would never keep the wardrobe.

I decided to go downstairs and tell the wardrobe to be good.

I quietly walked down the stairs. Then I stopped in surprise. The wardrobe wasn't making any noise. It was standing quietly next to the grandfather clock.

There was another *crash*. It came from the family room.

I was very scared, but I tiptoed to the door of the sitting room and peeped in. A man wearing a mask was putting things into a sack. There was a broken vase on the floor, and a chair was knocked over too. Those must have made the crashing sounds.

The man put Dad's camera into his sack, and then Mom's silver clock.

He was stealing our things! I felt very angry, but I didn't dare go in. Instead, I ran to the magic wardrobe.

"Wardrobe!" I whispered. "There's a burglar! Catch him!"

The wardrobe hurried into the family room on its little legs. I heard a scuffling noise. Then the burglar came running out with the sack on his back.

"Wardrobe!" I cried. "Help! Get the burglar!"

The wardrobe came running very fast out of the family room. It chased after the burglar and grabbed him with its wooden hands.

"What?" shouted the burglar. He looked very surprised. He wriggled and hit the wardrobe, trying to get free, but its hands were super strong. Then the wardrobe doors flew open and it stuffed the burglar inside itself. Its doors slammed shut and the key turned.

71

The burglar was locked inside the wardrobe.

"Yay!" I cheered. "Good work, Wardrobe!"

Seconds later, Mom and Dad appeared on the stairs. Mom was yawning, and Dad's hair was sticking up.

"I've had enough!" Dad said.

"What trouble has that wardrobe been getting into *now*?" Mom asked.

"No trouble," I told them. "It caught a burglar. It's a very, very *good* wardrobe."

When the police arrived, Dad opened the wardrobe doors. The police looked very surprised to see a burglar inside. They pulled

him out and put handcuffs on him. Then
they took all our things out of his sack and
gave them back to Mom.

The burglar was shocked. He told the police how the wardrobe had come to life and

trapped him, but they didn't believe him. Then the police took the burglar away. Mom made us some hot chocolate, and we all sat in the hall and looked at the wardrobe.

"You can't send it away now," I said. "You can't. It's a good, smart, brave wardrobe. It's part of the family."

I patted the wardrobe, and it patted me back.

"I know it is," Mom said, and she gave a yawn. "But it still needs training."

"I'll train it!" I said. "I'll look after it. Please? Please? It will be a really good wardrobe. I know it will."

Mom and Dad smiled at each other.

"Do you think you can do it, Ella?" Mom

asked. "It's a big job, training a magic ward-robe."

I thought about the wardrobe throwing out sweaters because they were itchy. I thought about it being lonely in the shed. I thought that if the wardrobe was really happy, maybe it would start being good all the time.

"Yes," I said. I sipped my hot chocolate and smiled back at Mom. "I think I can."

Fairy Spell #3

SPRINKLERIDOO!

Ice Cream for Everyone

We were going on vacation to Florida. There was going to be a beach and a swimming pool and boats to sail on. I had a new striped swimsuit, a new hat, and even a new red suitcase with wheels. Wardrobe was left in charge of the house while we were away. Even though he doesn't like magic very

much, Dad said Wardrobe would be better than any guard dog.

Before we left, Mom was having a lesson from Fenella on FairyTube. They were doing magic packing.

She waved her Computawand, pressed a code—*bleep-bleep-bloop*—and said, "Packeridoo!" But all the clothes whirled around the room and landed on our heads.

"Oops," Mom said. "Wrong code." She pressed a different number and tried again: "Packeridoo!"

At once all the clothes folded themselves neatly and put themselves in our suitcases. Magic is very useful sometimes.

When Mom's magic lesson was over, I said, "I wish I could do the Packeridoo spell every day, instead of having to pack my school bag. I wish I could do magic *now*."

"You'll be able to do it one day," Mom said, smiling. She gave me a hug, then said, "Have you packed your goggles?"

"Of course!" I said. "I'm going to swim every single day."

* * *

At the airport, it was very, very crowded. There were people and rolling suitcases everywhere. We couldn't see where to go. Dad went to ask someone, but it took him forever to come back. Ollie dropped his teddy and started crying. A man ran his suitcase over Mom's foot by mistake. More and

more people were arriving, and everyone was squashed. Mom looked annoyed.

"There are too many people here!" she said. "We'll never get to Florida!" She pulled us behind a luggage cart piled high with suit-cases so that no one could see. Then she stamped her feet three times, clapped

her hands, wiggled her behind and said, "Marshmallow," . . . and POOF! She was Fairy Mom.

She waved her Computawand at the crowds of people around us, pressed a code— *bleep-bleep-bloop*—and said, "Empteridoo!"

At once the airport was empty. There were no people or suitcases or carts. There were no check-in desks or signs. There were no planes outside.

There was no airport at all! Just a big empty building and our family. Dad came walking across the big, empty space. He rolled his eyes.

"Don't tell me," he said. "Magic."

"Oops," Mom said. "I don't know how *that* happened."

"There are no planes," I said, and I started crying. "Now we can't go on vacation!" I wouldn't be able to use my new suitcase or go swimming in my goggles.

"We *will* go on vacation!" Mom said, giving me a hug. "Don't worry, Ella. I will use magic to get the airport back."

"And then, maybe, put the Computawand away?" suggested Dad. "Just for a week."

When we got to our hotel, I was very excited. There was a beach and a swimming pool and a big jungle gym. There was a sandbox for Ollie and there were lots of lounge chairs to lie on.

The best lounge chairs were the blue ones by the sandbox. They had umbrellas with white fringe, and special tables and big comfy cushions. But another family had gotten them. They were French, and they all had dark hair. There was a mom and a dad and a girl and a baby boy—just like our family. They all wore sunglasses, even the baby. They looked very cool.

"Tomorrow we'll put our towels out early," Mom said, "so we can get those lounge chairs."

We swam and played all morning and I wrote a postcard to Tom and Lenka. Then, after lunch, I went to the sandbox. Ollie was playing with the French baby, and his sister was there too. She had a really nice swimsuit with flowers on it.

"Hello," I said. "I'm Ella."

"Allo," the girl said, with a French accent. "I am Cecile."

Cecile was older than me. She was twelve. We played together all afternoon and had loads of fun. Cecile could do back dives and

she could stand on her hands. We played diving for coins together and some-times she let me win, and then we had ice cream.

"Délicieuse!" said Cecile, licking her ice cream. "It mean . . . delicious!"

* * *

The next morning, I saw Mom on our balcony. She was holding all our beach towels, and she had turned into a fairy.

"Mom, what are you doing?" I asked. "Dad said no magic!"

"Shhh," she said. "Let's not wake him." She pressed a code on her Computawand—*bleep-bleep-bloop*—and pointed at the towels. "Towelseridoo!"

At once the towels flew off through the air. They looked like big birds with flappy white wings. I saw them land on the blue chairs by the sandbox.

"There," Mom said. "Now we will have the best spot."

"What if someone moves our towels?" I said.

"They can't," Mom said, giving me a wink. "Those towels have special magic now. No one can move them. Toffee apple!" And she was normal again.

But when we got down to the pool, our towels had moved. They were somehow on not-so-good lounge chairs instead. Cecile and her baby brother, Pierre, and their mom had the best lounge chairs.

Mom went up to Cecile's mom and said, "Excuse me. Our towels were on those lounge chairs."

Cecile's mom smiled. "Our towels are there now."

I knew Mom was annoyed, but she didn't want to show it. She came back to me and sat down on the not-so-good lounge chair. She looked at Cecile's mom.

I went and played with Ollie and Pierre in the sandbox. I helped them make a great big sand castle and then they both sat on it—*squash*. The whole time, I could see Mom thinking hard.

The next morning, before breakfast, I went onto the balcony again and saw Mom. She was watching the blue lounge chairs.

"Shhh," she said. "I'm waiting."

Then an amazing thing happened. Cecile's mom came out onto the balcony below, holding a pile of towels. She had shimmering wings, an emerald-green crown, and a Computawand. She was a fairy, just like Mom!

Cecile's mom pressed a code on her Computawand—*blum-blum-blam*—and said a word I didn't understand. At once

her towels flew through the air and landed on the best lounge chairs.

"I *knew* it!" Mom said. Very quickly, she stamped her feet three times, clapped her hands, wiggled her behind and said, "Marshmallow," . . . and POOF! She was a fairy.

She waved her Computawand at the towels. "Towelseridoo!"

The towels started flying back through the air. Cecile's mom couldn't believe her eyes. Then she looked up, saw Mom, and gasped something I didn't understand in French.

Mom shouted, "Towelseridoo!" again, and this time *our* towels started flying toward the best spot.

Cecile's mom yelled something else and her towels flew off too. They reached our towels and all the towels started

fighting in the air.
They were
wrestling, with
the corners
punching and
poking each other.

I couldn't stop laughing because they looked so funny. Then suddenly I saw an old man on the ground below. He was staring up at the fighting towels as though he couldn't believe his eyes.

"Careful!" I said. "That man is watching!"

"Oops," Mom said.

Cecile's mom looked guilty too.

They both called their towels back to the balconies. The two fairy moms stared at each other. Then they started laughing.

"We should share this spot," Cecile's mom said. "And be friends. My name is Marie."

That afternoon, Mom and Marie lay on their chairs next to each other. They talked and talked. Dad and Cecile's dad talked too. Mom and Marie showed each other their Computawands and told stories about when they were at Fairy School. The two dads talked about when magic spells go wrong. Marie's dad said that once Marie made the

Eiffel Tower disappear by mistake. My dad laughed and laughed.

Ollie and Pierre were playing together in the sandbox. I wanted to talk to Cecile, but she was busy reading a magazine.

"I like your swimsuit," I finally said.

"I made it with a magic spell." She looked around to check no one could see. Then she reached into her bag and pulled out a Computawand. "This is mine," she said. "Do you have one?"

I couldn't believe it. Mom always says I can't have my own Computawand until I'm grown up and graduate from Fairy School.

"No," I said. "I don't."

"You're not grown up enough yet," Cecile said with a smile. "Not like me. I can do lots of spells."

I instantly felt jealous. I wanted a Computawand like Cecile.

Then Mom came over. "Look, Cecile has a Computawand!"

Mom looked surprised too. "Goodness! In our country, children aren't allowed to have Computawands. It is against the Fairy Rule Book."

"But Cecile's not from here," I said. "Can I try hers?"

"No!" Mom said. She didn't look very happy. "Let's go down to the beach now."

We went down to the water and played in the waves and Dad pretended he was a shark. Ollie laughed and gurgled. But all I could think about was the Computawand. I really, *really* wanted to try it for myself.

* * *

After lunch, Mom and Dad went in the pool with Ollie. Cecile and Pierre were in the pool too, and so were their mom and dad. I was sitting on my lounge chair alone.

Cecile's bag was on the floor, and I could see her Computawand. I knew I shouldn't touch it. It wasn't mine. I wasn't allowed.

But maybe no one would notice if I did just one *tiny* spell.

I took the Computawand out. It was smaller than Mom's, but the buttons looked the same. When I touched it, it started to glow and grew into a wand. I can bring a Computawand to life because I am a Fairy in Waiting, but I'm not allowed to do magic. Whenever I play with Mom's Computawand, she turns off the magic function completely.

I tried to remember the codes Mom learned from her magic lessons with Fenella on FairyTube. I remembered the spell for a vanilla ice cream with sprinkles on top.

I knew I wasn't supposed to do any magic, especially with a Computawand that wasn't mine, but an ice cream cone would be yummy. If I ate it quickly, no one would know.

I pressed 4-3-2—*bleep-bleep-bloop*. Then I waved the wand and said,

"Sprinkleridoo!"

But nothing happened. I began to worry I had done the spell wrong.

Then I heard loud screams. I looked around and gasped. The pool wasn't blue anymore. It was filled with vanilla ice cream, with chocolate sprinkles sticking up every-where.

"Yay!" a boy nearby shouted. "An ice cream pool! This is the best vacation *ever!*"

Some children started licking the ice cream. Others dived into the pool with their

mouths open. Mom was holding Ollie in the shallow end and he started splatting ice cream into her face.

Everyone was slurping ice cream. One girl was trying to eat six chocolate sprinkles at once.

But soon everyone started getting out of the pool because they were too cold and they couldn't swim prop- erly. Pierre and Ollie started crying.

"This pool is freezing and icy!" an old man yelled angrily. "I want my money back!"

Suddenly Mom looked up at me. I still had the Computawand in my hand. I tried to hide it quickly, but Mom saw it.

"Ella!" Mom shouted. "What have you done?"

All the people in the pool were ice creamy and cold. I had ruined our vacation. I wasn't supposed to do magic. Mom would definitely be mad at me. I put Cecile's Computawand back in her bag as quickly as I could. Then I ran away, down to the beach, and I hid behind a lifeguard's chair. I wanted to hide forever.

* * *

When I heard Mom calling for me, I squeezed into a little ball. I didn't want her to find me. But she did. She sat down beside me and she took my hand.

"Oh, Ella," she said.

I started to cry, but I didn't look up.

"I ruined our vacation," I said.

"No you didn't," Mom said. "Don't worry. I always bring Fairy Dust on vacation, and so does Cecile's mom. We fixed everything."

"I'm sorry," I said in a tiny voice. "I wanted to be grown up and do spells on my own."

"You *will*," Mom said gently. "But not yet. You're too young for a Computawand. I never want you to touch one again, not even mine, unless I've said you can. Do you promise?"

"I promise," I said.

"Cecile was showing off," Mom said. "That wasn't her Computawand—it's an old one. Cecile is allowed to carry it, but she's not allowed to do spells. Her Mom is angry with her for fibbing."

"Oh," I said.

"Now tell me something," Mom said.

"What spell did you *want* to do?"

"I wanted a vanilla ice cream cone with sprinkles," I said.

"Good!" Mom said. "Look up, Ella."

I looked up. Mom was holding a vanilla ice cream cone with sprinkles.

"Here you are," she said, and she gave it to me. "You don't need to be a fairy to have an ice cream on vacation."

Mom hugged me and I hugged her back.

"Marie and I have decided to put away all our

Computawands," she said. "For the rest of vacation, we will just be two normal families. Do you think that's a good idea?"

I thought about Mom and the empty airport. I thought about the fighting towels. I thought about the ice cream swimming pool and all the freezing people. And I smiled at Mom.

"Yes," I said. "I think it's a very good idea."

Fairy Spell #4

FLYERIDOO!

The Best Birthday Party Ever

One morning I woke up to see Mom and Ollie standing by my bed with a bunch of balloons. For a moment I didn't know what was happening. . . . Then I remembered. It was my birthday!

"Happy birthday, sweetie!" Mom smiled, and she kissed me. "You have a very exciting day ahead of you. Waffles for breakfast, presents to open . . . and then this afternoon it's your party!"

"Weezi-weezi-weezi!" Ollie said, and he gave me a big smile with all his gums showing. I decided he meant "Happy birthday, Ella."

The party was in our living room. Mom had invited all my friends and made a pink cake and there was a magician. Mom explained to me that the magician couldn't do *real* magic like a fairy, only pretend magic. But it would still be fun.

It was a costume party too, so everyone was dressed up. I came as a clown and Lenka

came as an astronaut. Tom came as a caterpillar.

"I wish I really were an astronaut," Lenka
said. "I would fly to the moon."

"I would be a space caterpillar," Tom said.
"I would chase you around the moon."

"And I would be a space clown," I said,
"and fly around chasing you both!"

We all chased each other around the room,
making space-monster noises. Then my Not-
Best Friend Zoe arrived. She was dressed as a
princess, and she didn't join in the game. She
just stood by the door and gave us a horrible
look. Zoe is my Not-Best Friend because she
says mean things and pushes people. She
waits until the teacher isn't looking, and then

she shoves you and runs away. Mom says Zoe needs to grow up. I think Zoe just needs to stop being mean.

Mom and Dad were at the party too, dressed up like pirates. Aunty Jo was dressed as a

cat, with ears and a tail. Granny was dressed as Granny.

The magician started and we sat down to watch. But he wasn't a very good magician.

He made a coin disappear, but then he couldn't find it again. Then he did a trick

with cards, but he dropped all the cards on the floor, slipped on them and banged his head.

"Tragic," Aunty Jo said, shaking her head.

"Can't he do any better than that?" Granny added.

"Shhh!" Mom said. "You'll hurt his feelings."

The magician had a magic wand, but it didn't seem to work. When he said, "Abracadabra!" nothing happened.

The magician began to look very miserable. He moved on and tried to pull a rabbit out of a hat, but his trick didn't work—the hat was empty.

"I give up," he said, and sat down on the floor. "I can't find that rabbit anywhere."

All my friends were laughing at the magician. Even Tom was laughing. I started laughing too. The magician wasn't very good at magic, but he was funny.

"Do some magic!" Tom shouted at the magician.

"I'm trying to!" the magician said. "Magic is very hard!" He waved his wand, but nothing happened. "See?" he said.

"Very tragic," Aunty Jo said. She raised her eyebrows at Mom. "Normal humans shouldn't try to do magic."

"They said he was good on the website," Mom said, worried.

"The children don't mind," Dad said. He looked at his watch. "Is it time for cake yet?"

But Dad was wrong about people not minding, because my Not-Best Friend Zoe came over to me then. She was smiling, but in a mean way.

"This party is terrible," Zoe whispered. She said it quietly, in my ear. "It's really, really terrible."

"It's not," I said.

"Yes it is," Zoe said. "My party was much

better. At my party, we had go-karts and hot dogs. Your party is *terrible*."

"Excuse me?" A loud voice interrupted her. "This party is *not* terrible!" It was Mom, and she looked very fierce.

Zoe backed away. She looked a bit scared.

"This party is *not* terrible!" Aunty Jo agreed. She looked fierce too.

"No, it's certainly *not*!" Granny cried. She looked at Mom and Aunt Jo. "Can we?"

There was a pile of chairs at the side of the hallway. Granny, Aunty Jo and Mom all went behind the chairs, where no one could see them. They stamped their feet three times, clapped their hands and wiggled their behinds. I held my breath and watched them.

"Marshmallow!" Mom said.

"Strawberry shortcake!" Aunty Jo said.

"Extra-strong mint!" Granny said.

And . . . POOF! Suddenly all three were fairies with shimmering wings. Mom was wearing her silver crown, Aunty Jo Fairy was wearing her diamond crown and Granny Fairy was wearing her golden crown with blue stones. When you become a grown-up fairy, you choose your Fairy Crown and you have it forever. Mine is going to be pink and silver with diamonds all over.

Dad stared at them. "Really?" he said. "Is this a good idea? Everyone will see you!"

"They'll think we're in costume," Aunty Jo said.

"Just this once because it's Ella's birthday." Granny Fairy winked at me. Then she pointed at the magician with her star wand.

"Spelleridoo!" she shouted.

At once blue sparks came out of the magician's ears, then red puffs of smoke.

"Ooh!" everyone echoed.

The magician waved his magic wand and it played music.

He waved it again, and it made bubbles. He waved it again and candy came shooting out of the end.

"It's magic!" the magician cried. "I'm doing magic!"

The magician looked very excited. He started waving his wand everywhere. His toy rabbit turned into a real rabbit and started hopping around the floor. His cards built themselves into a tower, all by themselves. A string of handkerchiefs came out of his sleeve and started flying around the room like birds.

"This is amazing!" Lenka shouted.

"It's incredible!" Tom said, clapping.

Zoe didn't say anything, but she was watching with big, round eyes.

Then Aunty Jo waved her Computawand and shouted, "Flyeridoo!"

I could feel myself going up in the air. I felt like a bubble. I was flying! All my friends were flying too, and I heard them gasping and shrieking with excitement. It felt like

swimming in the air. We were all laughing
and kicking and waving at each other.

Dad and Mom were flying around holding hands. "This takes me back," he said. He
looked very happy. Sometimes I think Dad
only *pretends* not to like magic.

"Yahoo!" Tom shouted as he floated past
me. "This is the best party ever!" He started

kicking a helium balloon. "Let's play flying soccer!"

Everyone was flying and kicking the helium balloons. Ollie was flying upside down, saying "Weezi-weezi-weezi." The only person not flying was the magician. He was sitting on the floor, staring at his wand, saying, "Am I dreaming? Am I really, truly doing magic?"

Then I floated over toward Mom, Granny Fairy and Aunty Jo Fairy. They were standing by the table, looking at my pink birthday cake. Mom seemed a bit mad.

"What's wrong with it?" she asked
Granny Fairy and Aunty Jo Fairy.

"I made it myself."

"It could be bigger," Granny
Fairy said.

"And yummier," Aunty Jo
Fairy said.

"And grander," Granny Fairy said.

"With more icing and decorations," Aunty Jo Fairy said.

"Can I do it? I have a very
good Cake Spell. It won
a prize at the
Fairy Fair."

"No!" Mom said, looking even madder. "I'll do it!"

She pressed her Computawand—*bleep-bleep-bloop*—waved it in the air, and shouted, "Cakeridoo!"

At once the cake started to grow. It grew bigger and bigger and bigger.

"Stoperidoo," Mom said when the cake was as tall as me. But the cake didn't stop growing. "Stop!" Mom shouted. "Stoperidoo!"

But the cake still didn't stop.

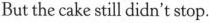

It grew so big it nearly reached
the ceiling. It was like a mountain
of cake, covered in pink icing
and pretty decorations. With
everybody flying in the air,
people started crashing
into it and pink icing
splattered everywhere.

I suddenly remembered one of Mom's magic lessons with Fenella on FairyTube. I flew up to Mom's ear and whispered, "Try saying, 'Stoperidoo, cakeridoo.'"

"Stoperidoo, cakeridoo!" Mom shouted, and at last the cake stopped.

"Yay, Mom!" I said quickly. "You did it!"

I wanted Granny and Aunty Jo to think

Mom was really good at magic, because she is. At least, sometimes.

"Now it's *too* big," Aunty Jo said.

"It's just right," I said. "I wanted a cake this big. Didn't I, Mom?"

"But everyone is stuck in the icing!" Granny Fairy said.

It was true. Everyone who had crashed into the cake was stuck. Now it was a pink cake decorated with my friends.

"Yum, yum, yummy!" Tom shouted. His whole face was covered in pink icing, and he was licking it off. "I love this birthday cake!"

Everyone was laughing and eating the icing and throwing icing snowballs at each other.

"It's the best cake ever," I said, and I gave Mom a hug.

"Did I make the cake grow too?" the magician asked. He looked shocked. "Am I really that good at magic?"

We all stood around the huge cake as Mom lit my candles and everyone sang "Happy Birthday." The cake was too big to cut, so everyone just pulled pieces off with their hands.

Then we all sat down, and the magician read us a story while Mom, Granny Fairy and Aunty Jo Fairy cleaned up the cake. Then Mom said, "Toffee apple!" Granny Fairy said, "Pancake!" and Aunty Jo Fairy said, "Blueberry pie!" and they were all normal again.

As the magician finished the story, Aunty Jo sprinkled Fairy Dust on him so that he would forget all about the magic he had seen. For ten seconds, the magician was very still. He had sort of gone to sleep. Then . . .

"Go!" Aunty Jo said, and he woke up.

"What happened?" he asked, blinking. "Is the party over? Did I do some magic? Did it work?"

"I don't think you should try to do magic anymore," said Aunty Jo. "It's not the job for you. Is there anything else you've always wanted to do?"

The magician sighed. "I've always wanted to be a train driver," he said. "Maybe I'll do that instead." He took his rabbit out of his bag and looked at me. "I won't need this rab-

bit anymore. Would you like it as a birthday present?"

"Yes! Yes, please!" I said. I crossed my fingers and toes and hoped Mom would say yes.

"All right, Ella," she said, smiling. "You can keep the bunny rabbit."

I was so, *so* happy. At last I had a pet of my own. I had a pet rabbit!

And then it was time for everyone to go home.

"This was the best party ever!" Tom said as he was putting on his coat. "Ever, ever, *ever.*"

"No it wasn't," Zoe said. "My go-karting party was the best."

"It wasn't," Tom said into my ear. "Yours was, Ella."

Zoe stared at me with small, mean eyes. She looked at me, then at Mom, Aunty Jo and Granny.

"How did you make everyone fly?" she asked. "How did your cake grow so big? Are you *magic* or something?"

I didn't know what to say. I'm not allowed to tell anyone that Mom is a fairy.

But luckily Granny heard Zoe. She came straight over and said, "It was the magician. He has lots of special tricks up his sleeve. Now go and get your party bag."

"But your mom had wings," Zoe said. "So

did your aunt and your granny. They looked like fairies. Are they real fairies?"

"They were costumes!" Aunty Jo said. "We're not really fairies, just like you're not really a princess."

Then Zoe's mom came in through the door and Zoe rushed over to her.

"Ella's mom was a fairy," Zoe said. "She was, she really was. She turned into a fairy. With wings."

"Wonderful, sweetie!" Zoe's mom said. "I love creative costumes."

"And we flew! And the birthday cake grew and grew. It was huge. They did magic. Real magic."

"That's great!" Zoe's mom said. "The magician must have been very talented. What a fun party. Have you said 'Thank you for having me'?"

Zoe got her party bag from Mom and she said, "Thank you very much for the party." Then she came up to me and looked at me again with her tiny, angry eyes. "I'm going to find out," she said in a quiet voice that no one else could hear. "I know your mom's a real fairy. And this birthday party only got good because of real magic. *Didn't it?*"

I thought about the magician and the blue sparks and the bubbles and the real rabbit. I thought about flying through the air, and the huge cake. I thought about everyone saying it was the best-ever birthday party. And I smiled.

"Thank you for coming, Zoe," I said. "I hope you had a great time."

FAMILY ACTIVITY GUIDE— FOR MORE FAIRY FUN!

UNSCRAMBLERIDOO!

Uh-oh! Ella borrowed Mom's Computawand and scrambled these words! Help solve the magical mayhem by unscrambling them. *(Answers on page 147.)*

★1 NFYCA SEDSR

_ _ _ _ _   _ _ _ _ _

★2 IFYRA TUDS

_ _ _ _ _   _ _ _ _

★3 TNO-BTES REIFDN

_ _ _ - _ _ _ _   _ _ _ _ _

FINDERIDOO!

Help Ella and her mom find Mrs. Lee's parrot!

(Answers on page 147.)

ICE CREAM RECIPE

You don't need a Computawand to make Ella's
favorite ice cream—make your own at home
with this simple recipe! Just make sure you ask a
grown-up to help, especially when using the whisk.
(You don't have to ask a fairy!)

INGREDIENTS

1 14-ounce can sweetened condensed milk
2 teaspoons pure vanilla extract
2½ cups heavy cream, cold

MORE FLAVORS

Chocolate: 9 tablespoons unsweetened cocoa powder
(½ cup + 1 tablespoon)
Strawberries: 1⅓ cup

1 Add the condensed milk, vanilla extract and cream to a large bowl. Add your cocoa powder or strawberries here too if you want to make different flavors!

2 Whisk the mixture for around 5 to 6 minutes, until soft peaks form.

3 Spread the mixture into a freezer-proof dish or tub. Cover and freeze for about 8 hours, until firm. Transfer to the fridge for 15 to 30 minutes before serving to soften.

What's YOUR Fairy Crown?

When girls become fairies,
they get to choose their own crown.
Draw your crown below.
Remember to color it in!

ANSWERS

UNSCRAMBLERIDOO!
(From page 142.)

 FANCY DRESS   FAIRY DUST   NOT-BEST FRIEND

FINDERIDOO!
(From page 143.)

About the Author

SOPHIE KINSELLA is a bestselling author. The adventures of Ella and Fairy Mom are her first stories for children. Her books for grown-ups have sold over thirty-eight million copies worldwide and have been translated into more than forty languages. They include the Shopaholic series and other titles, such as *Surprise Me, My Not So Perfect Life, Can You Keep a Secret?* and *The Undomestic Goddess,* and *Finding Audrey* for young adults.

Adults (including Fairy Moms everywhere) can follow her on social media:

🐦 @KinsellaSophie
📘 SophieKinsellaOfficial
📷 @sophiekinsellawriter